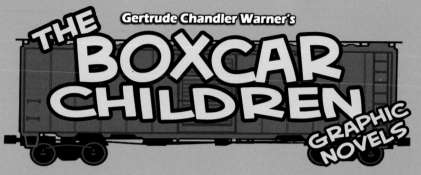

Gertrude Chandler Warner's

THE BOXCAR CHILDREN GRAPHIC NOVELS

TREE HOUSE MYSTERY

The Aldens have new neighbors, and they're helping them build a tree house! From up high they can see things they hadn't seen before. There's a strange round window on the house next door that's been hidden by trees—but nobody can find the window from inside the attic. Does their neighbor's old house have a secret?

THE BOXCAR CHILDREN
GRAPHIC NOVELS

THE BOXCAR CHILDREN
SURPRISE ISLAND
THE YELLOW HOUSE MYSTERY
MYSTERY RANCH
MIKE'S MYSTERY
BLUE BAY MYSTERY
SNOWBOUND MYSTERY
TREE HOUSE MYSTERY
THE HAUNTED CABIN MYSTERY

Gertrude Chandler Warner's

THE BOXCAR CHILDREN
TREE HOUSE MYSTERY

Adapted by Christopher E. Long
Illustrated by Mark Bloodworth

Henry Alden

Watch

Jessie Alden

Violet Alden

Benny Alden

Adapted by Christopher E. Long
Illustrated by Mark Bloodworth
Colored by Wes Hartman
Lettered by Johnny Lowe
Edited by Stephanie Hedlund
Interior layout and design by Kristen Fitzner Denton
Cover art by Mike Dubisch
Book design and packaging by Shannon Eric Denton

Library of Congress Cataloging-in-Publication Data
is available from the Library of Congress.

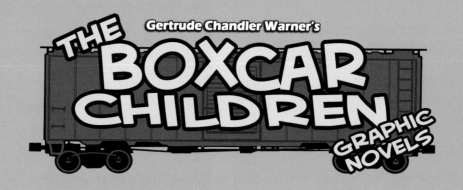

Gertrude Chandler Warner's

THE BOXCAR CHILDREN GRAPHIC NOVELS

TREE HOUSE MYSTERY

Contents

New Next Door…………………………………6

Benny's Plot………………………………..8

With Hammer and Nails…………………11

Up a Tree………………………………..13

Behind the Round Window………………..16

Mrs. McGregor's Clue……………………20

Good News……………………………..22

An Old Secret…………………………25

Lost and Found…………………………29

Henry, Jessie, Violet, and Benny Alden couldn't remember anyone ever living in the house next door.

Grandfather calls it the Beach House. I thought people spent summers there.

Mrs. McGregor knew the house from long ago.

An old lady lived there when I was a little girl. I wish I could remember more.

Well, there's a family there now.

There are two boys. I wonder how old they are.

We should go talk to them.

Benny yelled to get the new neighbors' attention.

Yoo-hoo! Welcome!

Thank you!

They're coming this way.

We're your new neighbors.

My name is Sammy Beach.

This is Jeffrey and Sammy. I'm sure they'll like living here.

We'll come over sometime when you get settled.

BENNY'S PLOT

Those kids next door are the weirdest boys ever.

Benny, that doesn't sound like you!

I'm just telling you the way it is. Grandfather, they don't play or do anything.

It's true. I've never seen boys like them.

One boy is ten and one is eight.

How do you know how old they are?

I asked them! Then I asked if they ever play, and they both said "no."

You have three weeks to learn about them. Then we leave on our family vacation!

We must do something for those boys.

Now what could we do? Let's think.

I know! A tree house! Everybody likes a tree house.

That's a great idea! Let's go find Jeffrey and Sammy.

Benny thought building a tree house would be fun.

My father has lots of tools!

We have lots of boards, too! I bet we could use them.

They found a great tree in the Beaches' yard.

This is the best tree in the whole yard.

It's a special tree. Dad and Uncle Max used to play in it.

Jeffrey and Sammy told the Aldens that their father and uncle grew up in the Beach House.

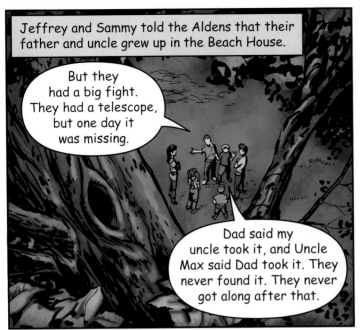

But they had a big fight. They had a telescope, but one day it was missing.

Dad said my uncle took it, and Uncle Max said Dad took it. They never found it. They never got along after that.

Now Uncle Max owns a restaurant not far from here.

That's Beach's Place. We should go there! We could ride our bikes.

I don't think we should start on the tree house until we ask your father and mother.

After all, it's their tree.

They all agreed to work on the tree house the next day, if Mr. and Mrs. Beach said it was okay.

WITH HAMMER AND NAILS

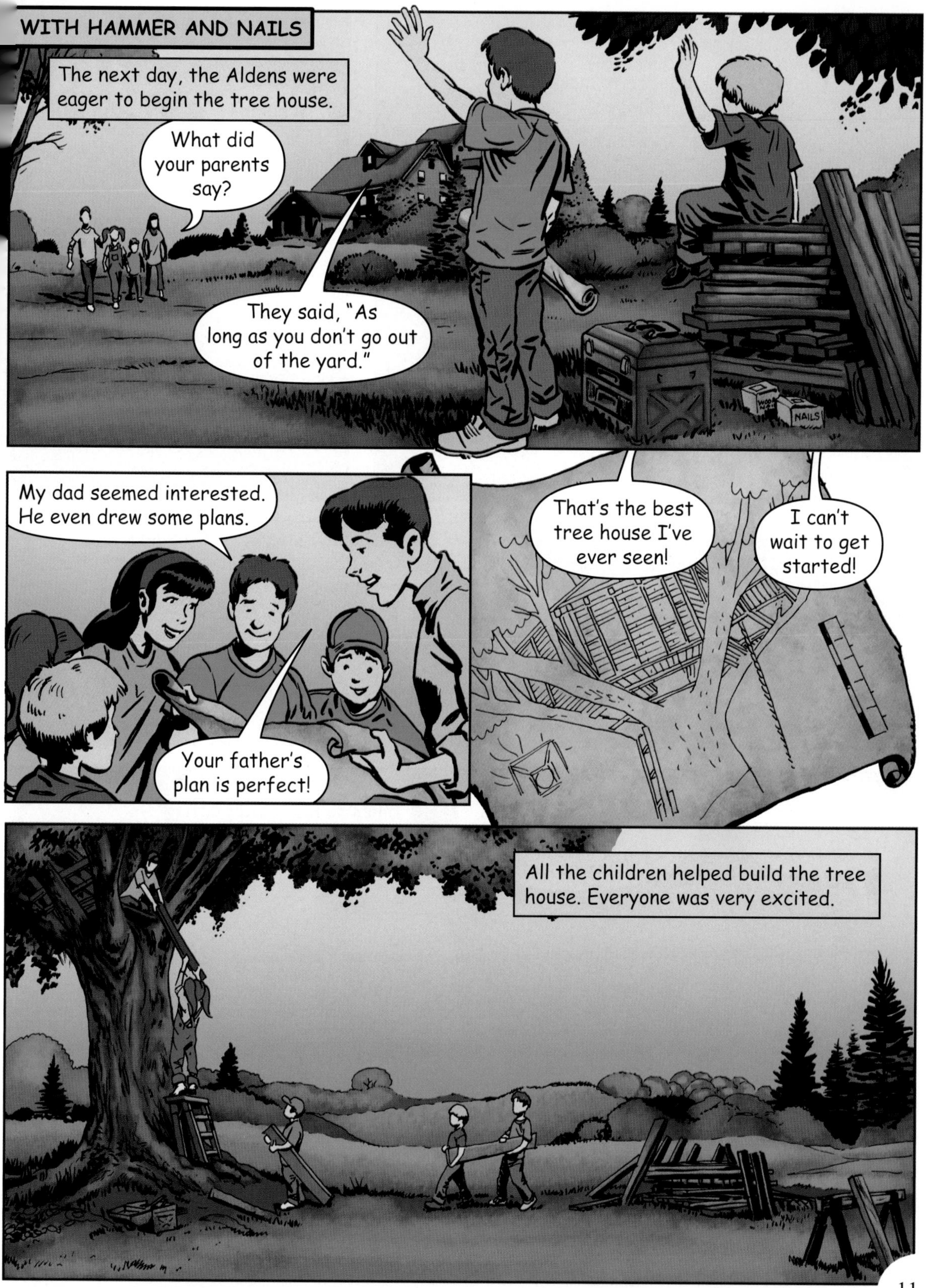
The next day, the Aldens were eager to begin the tree house.
What did your parents say?
They said, "As long as you don't go out of the yard."
NAILS
My dad seemed interested. He even drew some plans.
Your father's plan is perfect!
That's the best tree house I've ever seen!
I can't wait to get started!
All the children helped build the tree house. Everyone was very excited.

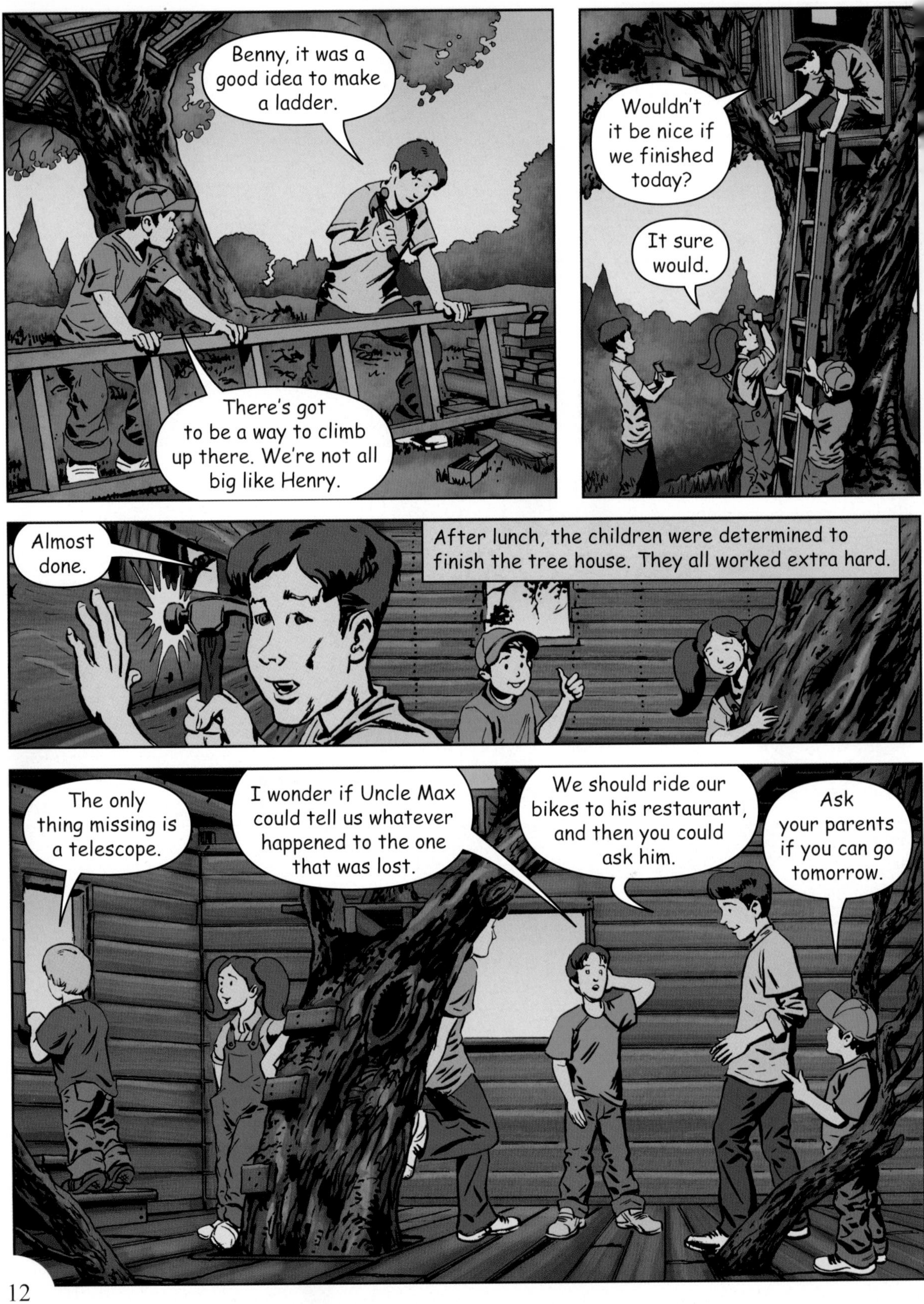
Benny, it was a good idea to make a ladder.
There's got to be a way to climb up there. We're not all big like Henry.
Wouldn't it be nice if we finished today?
It sure would.
Almost done.
After lunch, the children were determined to finish the tree house. They all worked extra hard.
The only thing missing is a telescope.
I wonder if Uncle Max could tell us whatever happened to the one that was lost.
We should ride our bikes to his restaurant, and then you could ask him.
Ask your parents if you can go tomorrow.

Mr. and Mrs. Beach agreed to let their sons ride their bikes to Uncle Max's restaurant. But only if they went with the older Alden children.

I can smell the food from here! I'm starving.

Uncle Max is a great chef.

Uncle Max was excited to see his nephews. Jeffrey and Sammy told him about the tree house. Then, they asked him about the telescope.

Your father and I had a tree house in that same tree. I haven't seen that telescope since then.

This is the best hamburger I ever had!

I sure wish other people knew that, Benny. My restaurant isn't doing very well.

Uncle Max wouldn't take a penny from the children. He loved seeing hungry people enjoying his food. The children thanked him and headed home.

Come back any time!

Thank you, Uncle Max!

Bye!

It rained the next day. Henry and Benny went to help Jeffrey and Sammy make a rope to pull them up into the tree house.

During the storm last night, I heard a rocking noise right above my bed. So I got Jeffrey.

I didn't hear anything. I told him it was just his imagination.

"But we went up to the attic to look around."

That sounds like a mystery.

It sure does!

The next day, Sammy made a discovery.

Hey, there's something in this tree!

Be careful, Sammy! It might be a squirrel, and they bite!

It's the lost telescope!

They must've put it in there and forgot about it.

That's great!

Hey! I see a round window. I haven't seen that before.

That's strange!

You can see the window from the tree, but not from the ground.

And it's not the attic window, because we didn't see it last night.

The mystery of the telescope is solved. But now there's the mystery of the round window!

Jeffrey and Sammy told their parents about the hidden window. Then, they went to investigate.

I think someone lived up on this floor. You can see nail holes for curtain rods.

Let's see what's in this closet.

Oh, look at the wallpaper! I've never seen anything like it.

16

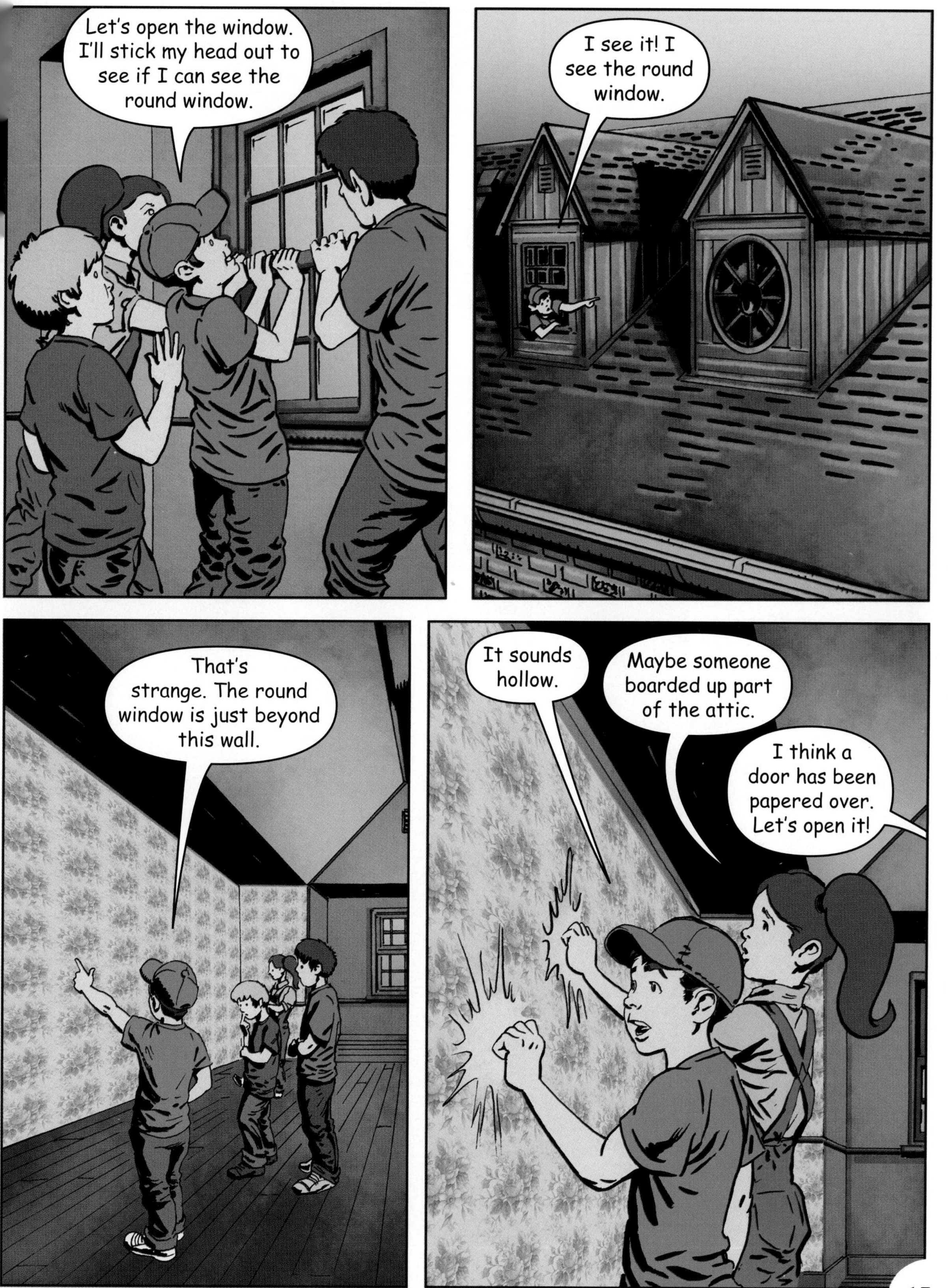
Let's open the window. I'll stick my head out to see if I can see the round window.
I see it! I see the round window.
That's strange. The round window is just beyond this wall.
It sounds hollow.
Maybe someone boarded up part of the attic.
I think a door has been papered over. Let's open it!

The children removed the wallpaper and found a door. They all wanted to see what was on the other side.

It was a boy's room.

This horse is what I heard the other night. The wind must blow in a little and make it rock.

Jeffrey and Sammy got their parents and showed them what they'd found.

I never knew a thing about this room.

Can we find out who the little boy was?

Uncle Max is older than I am. He might know. Let's go ask him tomorrow. And we'll tell him that you found the telescope.

Uncle Max was surprised that Sammy found the telescope. He and Mr. Beach apologized for being mad at each other.

Then, they told Uncle Max about the hidden room in the attic. They asked if he knew whose room it was.

I just know the Carver family built the house a long, long time ago.

Everyone loved the food and Beach's Place. They decided to think of a way to help attract more customers.

People don't use the road much anymore. You need to do something special to make them want to come here.

I could try a new name, but I don't know what it could be.

We'll come up with something!

Something great!

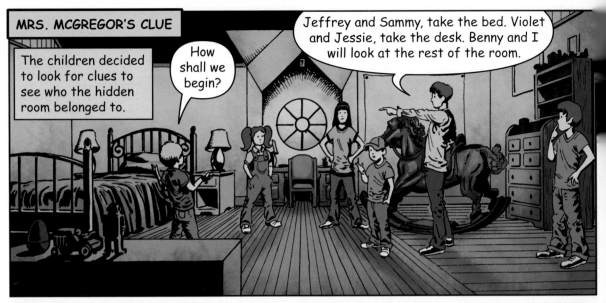

MRS. MCGREGOR'S CLUE

The children decided to look for clues to see who the hidden room belonged to.

How shall we begin?

Jeffrey and Sammy, take the bed. Violet and Jessie, take the desk. Benny and I will look at the rest of the room.

The children inspected the room carefully. But they couldn't find any clues until...

Hey, I found something.

The C must stand for Carver. But what about the W?

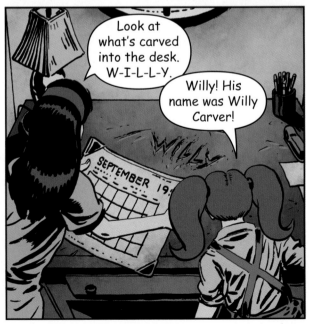

Look at what's carved into the desk. W-I-L-L-Y.

Willy! His name was Willy Carver!

SEPTEMBER 19

Mrs. McGregor listened as the children talked about Willy Carver.

I remember Willy Carver.

Really? Can you tell us about him?

When I was a little girl, I went to his birthday party. I think I remember what year it was, too.

A name and a date. That should help us.

My mom goes to the library to do research.

Maybe we should go the library, too.

After we eat some cookies.

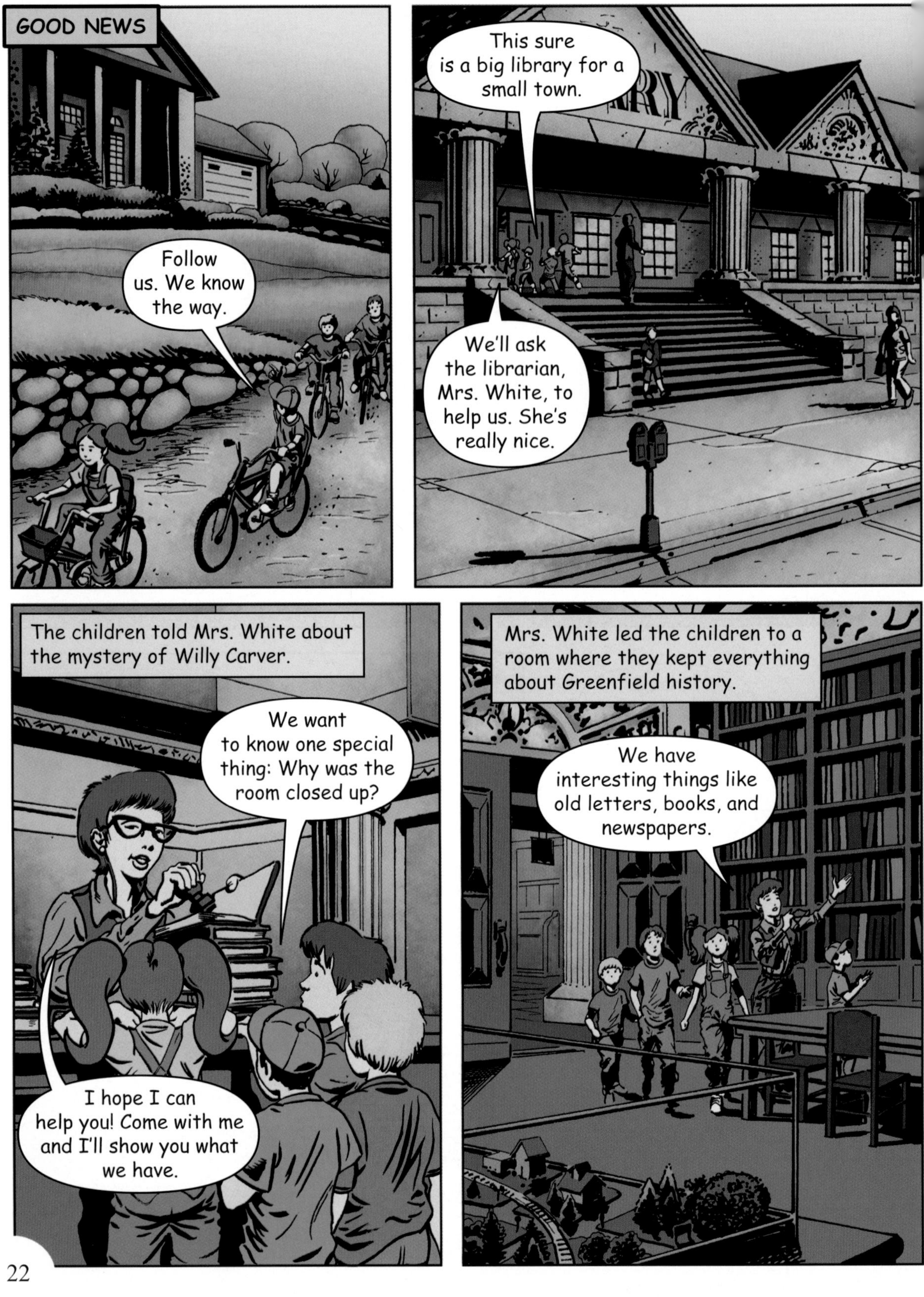
Follow us. We know the way.
This sure is a big library for a small town.
We'll ask the librarian, Mrs. White, to help us. She's really nice.
The children told Mrs. White about the mystery of Willy Carver.
We want to know one special thing: Why was the room closed up?
I hope I can help you! Come with me and I'll show you what we have.
Mrs. White led the children to a room where they kept everything about Greenfield history.
We have interesting things like old letters, books, and newspapers.

If the party was 50 years ago, I suggest looking though the newspapers. We made them into books for safekeeping.

Here it is.

Greenfield News
January 19_ to December 1_

Here! It says that Mrs. A.M. Carver is entertaining her grandson Willy for the summer.

It says that he's the son of Joseph Carver of London, England. He'll return to his parents in August.

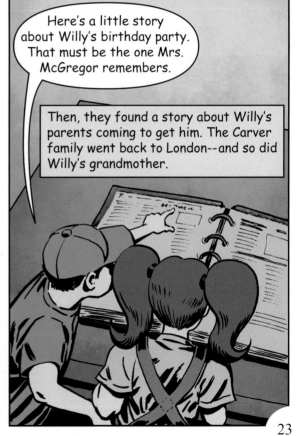

Here's a little story about Willy's birthday party. That must be the one Mrs. McGregor remembers.

Then, they found a story about Willy's parents coming to get him. The Carver family went back to London--and so did Willy's grandmother.

Now they knew what happened to the old woman and the boy. But what about the house?

"The Carver family home has been rented to Mr. and Mrs. David Johnson. They have five children."

Suppose Mrs. Carver didn't want strangers playing with Willy's toys. I'll bet she closed up that room so nobody would know it was there.

You may be right, Sammy.

The children knew they wouldn't find anything else about the mysterious room, because it was such a secret.

That night at dinner, Sammy had a stupendous idea.

Uncle Max could name his restaurant The Rocking Horse. We could give him the rocking horse for children to look at.

I would want to go to a place named The Rocking Horse.

So would I.

AN OLD SECRET

The next day, Sammy told Uncle Max about the newspaper stories about Willy Carver, Mrs. Carver, and the Johnsons.

Father bought the house from Joseph Carver. But I remember it had to be all cleaned up because so many children had lived there.

Uncle Max also recalled that a man with an English accent had come to see his father.

Father and the man went upstairs to look for something. But they didn't find it.

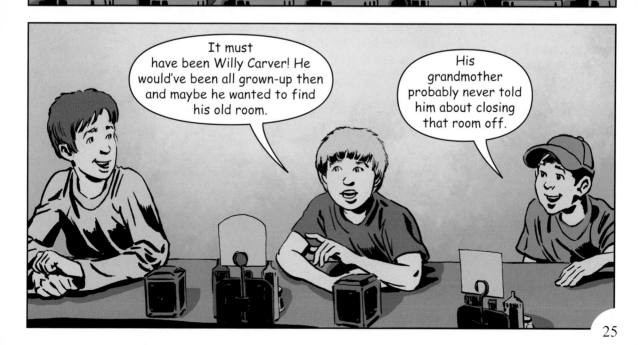

It must have been Willy Carver! He would've been all grown-up then and maybe he wanted to find his old room.

His grandmother probably never told him about closing that room off.

Now let's talk about your restaurant.

I haven't thought of a name yet.

I have! The Rocking Horse!

How did you ever think of it?

Sammy told Uncle Max about the rocking horse and all the other toys they found in Willy Carver's room.

We could bring the rocking horse here and put it by the door. And you could put the other toys on shelves around the room for children to look at.

I think everyone would like to see those interesting toys.

I can make a sign exactly like the old rocking horse. I'll have to see it first.

Come have dinner with us tomorrow and see the toys.

Everyone decided that they should have a barbeque for Uncle Max's visit.

Come on, Uncle Max!

We'll show you our tree house.

You're right. These toys are great.

Uncle Max showed them a book.

I thought I didn't have any clues, but I was wrong.

What is it, Uncle Max?

He told the children that the book had been in the house when they had first moved in.

I completely forgot about it. But I found it with my books and started to read it. It was Mrs. Carver's house journal.

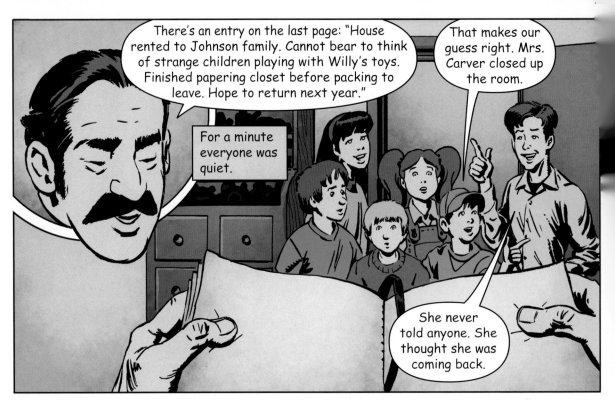

There's an entry on the last page: "House rented to Johnson family. Cannot bear to think of strange children playing with Willy's toys. Finished papering closet before packing to leave. Hope to return next year."

For a minute everyone was quiet.

That makes our guess right. Mrs. Carver closed up the room.

She never told anyone. She thought she was coming back.

And so the rocking horse has been hidden all this time!

I'm glad we're the ones who found it.

I am, too. And now it will have a new home and lots and lots of children will see it at my new restaurant.

There was plenty to do to help Uncle Max get his restaurant open.

Everyone helped.

The Rocking Horse Restaurant's big opening was the next day.

How does it look?

Stupendous!

I hope people come.

Oh, they will! I just know it!

And Benny was right. People did come. A lot of people!

There were so many customers, everyone helped Uncle Max, who was busy in the kitchen cooking food.

That's so cool!

This is the best food in town.

We'll have to come here again.

Everyone agreed that there were a lot of things lost. There was the telescope, the rocking horse, a whole room--and even Mr. Beach and Uncle Max's brotherly love.

Without the tree house, none of the things would have been found. And the entire Beach family was grateful that Henry, Jessie, Violet, and Benny had had the idea and helped build it.

ABOUT THE CREATOR

Gertrude Chandler Warner was born on April 16, 1890, in Putnam, Connecticut. In 1918, Warner began teaching at Israel Putnam School. As a teacher, she discovered that many readers who liked an exciting story could not find books that were both easy and fun to read. She decided to try to meet this need. In 1942, *The Boxcar Children* was published for these readers.

Warner drew on her own experience to write *The Boxcar Children*. As a child she spent hours watching trains go by on the tracks near her family home. She often dreamed about what it would be like to live in a caboose or freight car—just as the Alden children do.

When readers asked for more Alden adventures, Warner began additional stories. While the mystery element is central to each of the books, she never thought of them as strictly juvenile mysteries. She liked to stress the Aldens' independence. Henry, Jessie, Violet, and Benny go about most of their adventures with as little adult supervision as possible—something that delights young readers.

During her lifetime, Warner received hundreds of letters from fans as she continued the Aldens' adventures, writing nineteen Boxcar Children books in all. After her death in 1979, her publisher, Albert Whitman and Company, carried on Warner's vision. Today, the Boxcar Children series has more than 100 books.